The History
of Home

** bp**

Bilingual Press/Editorial Bilingüe

General Editor
Gary D. Keller

Managing Editor
Karen S. Van Hooft

Associate Editors
Ann Waggoner Aken
Theresa Hannon

Editorial Consultant
Janet Woolum

Editorial Board
Juan Goytisolo
Francisco Jiménez
Eduardo Rivera
Severo Sarduy
Mario Vargas Llosa

Address:
Bilingual Review/Press
Hispanic Research Center
Arizona State University
Tempe, Arizona 85287
(602) 965-3867

The History
of Home

Leroy V. Quintana

Bilingual Press/Editorial Bilingüe
TEMPE, ARIZONA

ISBN 0-927534-36-3

Library of Congress Cataloging-in-Publication Data

Quintana, Leroy.
    The history of home / by Leroy V. Quintana.
        p. cm.
    ISBN 0-927534-36-3 (pbk.)
    I. Title.
    PS3567.U365H57 1993
    813'.54—dc20   93-10204
                                           CIP

PRINTED IN THE UNITED STATES OF AMERICA

Cover design by Kerry Curtis

Back cover photo by Elisa V. Quintana

Acknowledgments

Funding provided by a grant from the National Endowment for the Arts in Washington, D.C., a Federal agency.

Grateful acknowledgment is given to the following periodicals in which some of these poems have appeared:

Blue Mesa Review 2 (Spring 1990), *Confluencia* 4.1 (Fall 1988), and *Zyzzyva* 6.3 (Fall 1990).

Contents

Introduction

Leroy V. Quintana's
Return and Search for the Center

Antonio C. Márquez
University of New Mexico

> "Trying to find my way back to the center of
> the world where Grandfather stood that day"
> (*Sangre*[1])

New Mexican poetry is part and parcel of Chicano literature. The literature of New Mexico shares the general characteristics of Chicano literature, and at the same time its
particular history and literary traditions have carved out a
niche. Bruce-Novoa offers a pertinent clarification:

> A desire to document the life of one's commu-
> nity is characteristic of Chicano writing. It re-
> sponds directly to the absence, or falsification, of
> that life in the written record presented by the
> dominant culture. . . . In this light Chicano litera-
> ture can be seen as a rewriting of U.S. history to
> include the Chicanos, whose story has been
> passed orally. . . . New Mexican Chicanos employ
> this strategy also. If anything, they have an even
> stronger sense of historical pride and the need to
> rewrite the record because they can rightfully
> claim a much longer continued presence in what
> is now the United States than any other group
> save Native Americans.[2]

To be sure, Native Americans sang paeans to the land
long before the Spanish *conquistadores* arrived. In the six-
teenth century those songs were cast in new voices and a
new language. It started on January 8, 1598, when the Juan
de Oñate expedition arrived in New Mexico with 129 colonists. They brought with them a literary tradition as part of
their cultural baggage, and it marked the start of Hispanic-
Mexican poetry. Among Oñate's soldiers was Gaspar Pérez
de Villagrá; he was to write *Historia de la Nueva México*

3

(published in Spain in 1610), which is considered the first history of any American commonwealth and the first American epic.[3] Planted and seeded by these first explorers and colonists, folklore and popular culture flourished. An oral tradition was established, one that admirably suited the needs of the people and provided an avenue to express their everyday experiences. Rowena Rivera, a folklorist and student of Southwest colonial literature, pinpoints the significance:

> In fact, what gave resiliency and flexibility to Spanish/Mexican colonial oral poetry was precisely its bond to the reality of the common folk. As such it was therefore always suitable to be used in any way that it was needed, so long as it adhered to the community's religious ideology, its code of ethics, its sense of aesthetics, and its own literary canons.[4]

Miguel de Quintana (1670-1747) exemplifies the wellsprings of New Mexican poetry. Quintana perpetuated the oral tradition, produced a body of excellent poetry, and bequeathed a legacy to contemporary Chicano poetry. Colahan and Lomelí's "Miguel de Quintana: An Eighteenth-Century New Mexico Poet Laureate?" convincingly argues the case for this extraordinary poet and important historical figure:

> Quintana's work is also of particular interest as an antecedent to the distinctive form of Hispanic literature existing in what is now the Southwest of the United States. . . . His determined and outspoken resistance, drawing strength from his neighbors' support and from traditional elements of Hispanic lore, shows an undeniable connection with the thrust of much of contemporary Chicano literature.[5]

A vibrant literary current extends from Miguel de Quintana to Leroy V. Quintana; patronymic similarities apart, it is a spiritual bloodline that celebrates the "land of enchantment."

The prefatory lines from the concluding poem in *Sangre*, aptly titled "Legacy," bridge to Quintana's latest volume of poetry, *The History of Home*, which continues the exploration of the past and Quintana's attempt to recapture the center created long ago by family and culture. That center is a locus of multiple metaphors and connotations: home, family, religion, childhood, innocence, hope, and love. The poem "Judy, Judy, Judy" explicitly states the central theme and Quintana's tack: "So long ago, a place called home I think about / now and then, often, today and today also. . . . " Specifically, the poem turns to a place where love was given, however fleetingly, and is now retrieved through memory and poetic introspection: "She was one of the few who ever loved me there." To someone unfamiliar with Quintana's work, the first impression might be that his poetry is simple, quaint, or sentimental. Although Quintana can coin poignant refrains on remembrances of things past, his work is not mired in moony nostalgia. Neither his work nor his life has been easy, simple, or frivolous. In fact, both merge into an aesthetic and existential search for a purposeful center of things, and a bittersweet but compassionate voice breaks through stones of silence to utter truths that have been felt and perhaps now and then also denied.

Leroy V. Quintana was born in Albuquerque, New Mexico, on June 10, 1944. His formative years were spent with his grandparents in Raton, New Mexico (the story telling source of much of his poetry), and he moved back and forth between grandparents and parents throughout his childhood. In 1952, his parents settled permanently in Albuquerque; the next ten years Quintana attended parochial elementary schools and Albuquerque High School (the city's oldest and most racially mixed school). For two years following high school he learned his father's trade and worked as a roofer. Leaving the trade of roofing for university studies, he studied at the University of New Mexico from 1964 to 1967, majoring in anthropology. In 1967, he volunteered for the army; he passed muster for airborne duty and served a year in Vietnam. His experiences and those of other Chicanos in Vietnam would become the subject of his most angry poems: a cycle of seventeen poems titled "What Can They Do, Send Us to The Nam?" and *Interrogations,* published in 1992. After his two-year stint in the army, Quintana resumed his studies at the University of New Mexico, this time majoring in English. At the same time, he worked at St. Joseph's Alcoholic Treatment Center, starting his career in mental health and counseling. From 1972 to 1974, he worked on his M.A. in English and was a teaching assistant at New Mexico State University. Upon receiving his degree, Quintana joined the faculty of El Paso Community College and taught there for five years. His first volume of poetry, *Hijo del pueblo: New Mexican Poems,* was published in 1976. Two years later he won a National Endowment for the Arts creative writing fellowship. In 1980, he returned to Albuquerque. He taught part-time at the University of New Mexico and started a new career as a journalist, writing feature and sports articles for the *Albuquerque Tribune.* Straddling two vocations, Quintana published his second volume of poetry, *Sangre,* in 1981. *Sangre* brought critical recognition and earned him a significant place in contemporary Chicano poetry. Quintana shifted careers again; from 1982 to 1984 he studied and received his master's degree in counseling from Western New Mexico University. Quintana left his native New Mexico for San Diego in 1984 to work as a marriage, family, and child counselor at the San Ysidro Mental Center until 1988. The past two years, Quintana has been an instructor of English at Mesa Community College in San Diego. With his return to academia, Quintana has returned to teaching literature and writing poetry. In both respects, it is a joyful return and cause for celebration.

Quintana's life experiences as small-town boy, Catholic schoolboy, barrio *vato,* college student, grunt in Vietnam and returning veteran, husband, father, journalist, activist, psychiatric counselor, and teacher greatly inform his poetry. Taking into account the licenses and creative means of poetry, Quintana's art is a poetry of experience, and it is extracted from historical and personal facts. Quintana broaches the subject in an interview: "I guess I had a private code about my writing. I always told myself that whatever I wrote had to be honest, so all the characters are true to life."[6] His avenue to versimilitude has been the oral tradition, which is the genesis and sustaining source of his poetry. Starting with Américo Paredes's seminal study, "The Folk Base of Chicano Literature," literary historians have amply documented and established the essential role of the oral tradition in the development of Chicano literature. Santiago Daydí-Tolson's critical introduction to *Five Poets of Aztlán*, an anthology that contains thirty-six of Quintana's poems, reiterates the influence of popular culture and underscores its importance in defining Chicano poetry: "The authenticity of this appropriation of an oral and popular tradition is undeniable: it does not function as a mere decorative reference to the ethnic past, as some nativist works used to do in other Latin American settings, but it exists as the poem itself—it constitutes its vision and its words."[7] This base has a special bearing for writers such as Sabine R. Ulibarrí, Rudolfo A. Anaya, Denise Chávez, Leo Romero, and Leroy V. Quintana. Their writings are deeply rooted in the oral tradition of New Mexico and inspired by a sense of place. Although Quintana now lives in California, New Mexico remains his cultural bedrock: "I still see a lot of New Mexico influence in the poetry that I've done. . . . It's all New Mexican at the core. I don't think that I'll ever be anything else."[8] Sabine R. Ulibarrí, the dean of New Mexican writers, describes the attachment to the land and the inspiring cultural legacy:

> New Mexico is our native land, our fatherland
> and motherland. . . . we have a language, a his-
> tory, and a tradition that knit and hold us to-
> gether in a manner that cannot be matched by
> any other minority group. . . . Our roots run deep
> and sinuous in the land of our forefathers. Our
> culture is based on the soil. We have a running
> and ancient dialogue going with the mountains
> and the mesa, the sunsets and the deserts, the

paisano and the ponderosa, the wail of the coyote and the lament of la llorona.[9]

Like Ulibarrí, Quintana has lived in northern New Mexico, a region noted for its spectacular natural beauty, rugged and proud people, and a perdurable Hispanic culture.

Quintana succinctly and charmingly states the case: "In many ways, I'm still basically a smalltown New Mexican boy carrying on the oral tradition."[10] We should not be led astray by his self-effacement. Quintana is a learned man, and he can knowledgeably discuss Yeats, Joyce, Eliot, Pound, Stevens, García Lorca, Neruda, and a host of other authors. However, his self-placement in the oral tradition is correct and informative. But Quintana is not a simple man or self-satisfied poet; on occasion he has testily questioned the traditional influences on his work ("I think I got caught up too much in the New Mexico oral tradition stuff") and he is self-conscious of being locked in formulaic story poems. Thus, Quintana is experimenting with a fragmentary, modernistic style in his Vietnam manuscript, *Interrogations*. Despite his autocriticism and experimentation with other forms, he acknowledges the difficulty—and perhaps the inadvisability—of extricating himself from the oral tradition:

> I *do* come out of that tradition. I remember grandmother making candy on the old firewood-burning stove and telling us all the old cuentos deep and long into the night . . . grandfather telling me tales of walking to Wyoming and shepherding as a kid along with all the traditional cultural stuff. So it's very difficult. . . . And as I say, that tradition is so ingrained in me. . . . I heard grandmother tell me the old stories hundreds of times, over and over. . . . You know, that seems to be lost, and I would hope that I could at least put a little bit of that on paper, although I would, I think, be very grandiose in saying that I have accomplished what I would like to.[11]

In a larger context, Quintana joins the concerted efforts of many Chicano and Chicana writers who want to preserve aspects of traditional culture, moved by the necessity of salvaging them before they are totally lost. Cordelia Candelaria's valuable study, *Chicano Poetry: A Critical Introduction* (1986), neatly summarizes Quintana's participation in the preservation of culture: "Quintana's poetic lens is more documentary as it seeks to picture and preserve (at least in art) the life and habits of a culture that has resisted the encroachment of modernity and anglicization."[12] Candelaria's parenthetical expression is, of course, the heart of the matter. The oral tradition is the cornerstone of Quintana's art and the stories he heard from the *viejitos* have provided the grist for his best poems.

A fine example of how Quintana continues the oral tradition and converts familial storytelling into an engaging story-poem can be found in "Sangre 4." He takes the story line mentioned above, of his grandfather walking to Wyoming and shepherding there, and expands it to make a poignant statement on leaving home and dying unmourned among strangers. "Grandfather had a little brother, Enrique, / who walked with him all the way to Wyoming / to shear sheep and never returned" (6). The family receives the news that Enrique was murdered for his money on the way home, beaten to death in a bar in Pueblo, Colorado. The grandfather is torn between claiming and returning his brother's body at considerable expense or using the money to feed his family. His decision and the consequences lend the poem a haunting quality:

> I am told grandfather was filled with regret
> over the fact he did not go back,
> and was haunted for the rest of his days,
> knowing he had left Enrique behind, and alone
> forever somewhere in a potter's field in Pueblo. (6)

"I am told" fixes the frame of the oral tradition, but the emotional undercurrent of the poem is solely of Quintana's device. Moreover, masterful understatement carries a profound comment on the anguished decisions and tragic limitations that are a part of poverty. This poem validates Daydí-

Tolson's observation on the subtle characteristics of Quintana's poetry: "Quintana is a master of nuances and likes to avoid the overly manifest in favor of the suggestive touch or almost invisible sharp edges, sometimes all the more eloquent for their lingering effect."[13]

The best work in *The History of Home* has a similar clarity, precision, and evocative force. Also, Quintana stays with his forte and reworks favorite themes and motifs. The *cuento* or folk narrative can take different forms (e.g., anecdote, legend, fable, myth, parable) and assumes the most appropriate or effective voice (e.g., comic, satiric, lyrical, moralistic, or accusatory). Quintana's story-poems touch base with these forms and voices. Thematically, the poems in *The History of Home* can be placed in these subject categories: (1) family portraits and family history; (2) nonfamilial but memorable characters and events (these experiences focus on parochial education, childhood friends, schoolyard antics, and childhood exploration of sex and the mysteries of love); (3) juxtaposition of the past and later years, pairing childhood and adulthood, and contrasting innocence with the experience and acquired wisdom of the years.

A recurring theme that connects *The History of Home* with previous volumes is Quintana's sardonic treatment of progress and the changes that beset Chicano communities and their traditional life-styles. Douglas K. Benson, who has provided the best critical work on *Hijo del pueblo* and *Sangre,* underscores this aspect of Quintana's poetry:

> Quintana has begun to open up for us this complex, hermetic New Mexican world, difficult to penetrate for an urbanized, technologically oriented readership. . . . a world which shows us the interfaces between it and our modern view of things while at the same time offering as a response and a weapon against this other world of ours which seems to wish to negate our very humanity in its rush to be "efficient."[14]

I hasten to add that Quintana's poetry does not fall within a body of sentimental literature that cloyingly depicts a pastoral New Mexico. If anything, Quintana's sharp irony and acute vision counter the romantic claptrap that has been expended on New Mexico.

Of course, skepticism or the repudiation of an industrial-technological order is a commonplace of modern poetry. In Chicano poetry, the vagaries of progress become a pressing concern because of the assimilationist forces exerted by the dominant culture and the threatened erosion of traditional Chicano culture. To this end, Quintana employs antithesis and shapes contrasting movements from outer to inner elements. The poem "Arturo" is an apt example. Recalling the dizzy, momentous events of 1958, Quintana comically juxtaposes the outside forces with a community stock figure, the impervious chile-stained Arturo:

> When the Russians put Sputnik in space
> we were in the seventh grade
> The world beginning to rock, crazy
> as Jerry Lee Lewis on the piano:
> "A Whole Lotta Shakin' Goin' On."
> One of the few sure things left
> was Arturo coming back to school from lunch
> every day with red chile stains
> on both corners of his mouth.

Clearly, the movement of the poem is from the outside to inside, from the outer world of ballistics technology and rock 'n' roll to the inner world of community experience. The mundane and familiar experience is not so much in the comic portrait of Arturo; rather, the warm-hearted jest rests on the things that remain constant, such as the delicious staple of the New Mexico Chicano diet and the tell tale signs of eating red chile.

The latest volume again discloses Quintana's marvelous sense of humor; at its best, his comic manner is hilarious and exactingly witty. On the other hand, there is also a profound seriousness in Quintana, and it engenders his most effective and engaging poems. *The History of Home* contains a series of poems that evoke "la tristeza de la vida," and Quintana covers the gamut: racism, injustice, poverty, war, alienation, emotional death, despair, loneliness, madness, and death. The moralistic or accusatory perspective is prompted by Quintana's reflections on human suffering and the cruel ironies of life. The story of "Patty," a childhood friend and a loser for life, is a litany of lost hopes and endless misfortune: "She had learned about cheated hopes, corruption / anguish, and upheaval long before there was a country / in southwest Indochina, divided." The same poignancy laces the memories of "Teddy," a sensitive lad and music lover whose appreciation ranged from Bach to Charlie Parker, but descended into madness and inexplicable matricide: "Next day I didn't have to read past the *Tribune* headlines / to know it was he who had beaten / his mother to death with a hammer in 5/4 time." These poems and similar ones manifest the brooding, darker side of Quintana's poetic vision.

Quintana's acute sensibility is most evident in the final poem, a mournful remembrance of John F. Kennedy's assassination—and the repercussions. It evokes the fateful day that shattered dreams and left some in a maelstrom of confusion and despair. Quintana took risks with this poem; it could have slid into "What were you doing the day JFK was shot?" gimcrack. Instead, Quintana nerves the poem by shifting focus to the construction workers, including the most exploited labor force in the country:

> My stepfather climbed back up the ladder,
> said a black man, a carpenter, told him he'd lost a friend.
> He shook his head sadly,
> not knowing what else or more to say.
> We went back to work, the world now coming apart.
> And all the men, and all the nails,
> and all the Mexican wetback bricklayers
> at a penny a brick,
> could never put it back together again.

Quintana furbishes the Yeatsian trope—"Things fall apart / the centre cannot hold"—admixing the historic and the quotidian and rendering the speechless, heartfelt grief of the community. The irony is inescapable; the workers are building shelters for a nation, but no on˄ can construct or restore the lost hope and failed dream. The placement of the poem gives it added significance: it comes back to Quintana's search for the center—a place of order, harmony, purpose, and communal values. It is indicative of a poet who cares for humanity and our collective survival in the face of a "world now coming apart." Ultimately, Quintana's poetry is about what has been deeply felt and known, and the acquired wisdom of the years shines through in lapidary poems that offer brief but honest, true, and kind illuminations.

In 1976, Keith Wilson eloquently praised Quintana's first volume of poetry, *Hijo del pueblo*: ". . . just a quick shadow of fear for the mountains' darkness, the long winters of the hill country, the laughter and the deaths of the old and of the children. It's all here—*puro Nuevo México*—in the high quiet of these fine poems." Seventeen years later and many poems in between, Quintana remains *un hijo del pueblo*. His love for the land and its people has not been exhausted— nor has the gifted means to express the enduring attachment. His work is still *puro Nuevo México,* and Chicano culture is still part and parcel of Quintana's life and poetic vision.

Notes

[1]Leroy V. Quintana, *Sangre* (Las Cruces, NM: Prima Agua Press, 1981), 24.

[2]Bruce-Novoa, "New Mexican Chicano Poetry: The Contemporary Tradition," *Pasó por aquí: Critical Essays on the New Mexican Literary Tradition, 1542-1988,* ed. Erlinda Gonzales-Berry (Albuquerque: University of New Mexico Press, 1989), 270.

[3]Luis Leal, "The First American Epic: Villagrá's History of New Mexico," *Pasó por aquí,* 47.

[4]Rowena A. Rivera, "New Mexican Colonial Poetry: Tradition and Innovation," *Pasó por aquí,* 83-84.

[5]Clark Colahan and Francisco A. Lomelí, "Miguel de Quintana: An Eighteenth-Century New Mexico Poet Laureate?" *Pasó por aquí,* 66.

[6]Douglas K. Benson, "A Conversation with Leroy V. Quintana," *Bilingual Review/Revista Bilingüe*, vol. 12, no. 3 (1985): 221.

[7]Santiago Daydí-Tolson, "Voices from the Land of Reeds," *Five Poets of Aztlán*, ed. Santiago Daydí-Tolson (Binghamton, NY: Bilingual Press/Editorial Bilingüe, 1985), 19.

[8]Benson, "A Conversation with Leroy V. Quintana," 228.

[9]Reynaldo Ruiz, "Sabine R. Ulibarrí," *Dictionary of Literary Biography, Vol. 82: Chicano Writers. First Series*, eds. Francisco A. Lomelí and Carl R. Shirley (Detroit: Gale Research Inc., 1989), 266.

[10]Douglas K. Benson, "Leroy V. Quintana," *Dictionary of Literary Biography, Vol. 82*, 200.

[11]Benson, "Conversation with Leroy V. Quintana," 222.

[12]Cordelia Candelaria, *Chicano Poetry: Critical Introduction* (Westport, CT: Greenwood Press, 1986), 190.

[13]Santiago Daydí-Tolson, "Voices from the Land of Reeds," 37.

[14]Douglas K. Benson, "Intuitions of a World in Transition; the New Mexico Poetry of Leroy V. Quintana," *Bilingual Review/Revista Bilingüe*, vol. 12, nos. 1 & 2 (1985): 78.

The History
of Home

dedicated to
Fileberto Jaramillo

.

GUADALUPE

If I had lived the rest of my life in that small town
she's the one I would have married, I'm sure. Guadalupe,
with long, black hair. Guadalupe,
as dark as I was. Guadalupe,
who one day came walking up the dirt road,
past Grandfather's house and smiled and my heart—
Oh, she was beautiful! The most beautiful
girl in school! I could tell she liked me—
my fourth-grade heart unbelieving.
If I had lived the rest of my life in that small town
she's the one I would have married, I'm sure.
As sure as I dreamed back then I would play for the
Yankees
and come back home a hero.

SEVEN-FOOT PICKETT

I wish I could have been there before school that day
when Seven-Foot Pickett stopped by the playground
campaigning, again, for State Corporation Commissioner.
The only things in sight taller were the flagpole,
the smokestack down at the Santa Fe Railroad shops.

JUDY, JUDY, JUDY

I wonder what happened, whatever happened
to that girl Judy, Judy was her name,
who would follow me, would follow me after school
determined, so determined for a kiss, just a kiss.
She was coy, pretended to be coy and was
perhaps, perhaps a little.
I supposed I teased her, yes, I teased her.
Truth is I wanted her, wanted her just as much,
as much.
Oh, I could have, oh, so easily, so easily.
My hands over, or even under, the blouse
of her Catholic school uniform,
touched
her breasts, small but not too, for a seventh grader.
Jesus, Jesus, Jesus, Judy, Judy, Judy.
So long ago, a place called home I think about
now and then, often, today, and today also about Judy,
and how she was one of the few who ever loved me there.

ARTURO

When the Russians put Sputnik in space
we were in the seventh grade.
The world beginning to rock, crazy
as Jerry Lee Lewis on the piano:
"A Whole Lotta Shakin' Goin' On."
One of the few sure things left
was Arturo coming back to school from lunch
every day with red chile stains
on both corners of his mouth.

SARAH

Sarah came to our school in the seventh grade.
All the boys liked her instantly, of course.
We had a dance, and she refused everybody.
Well, I'd show her, pulled her out onto the floor.
So, like good Catholic school girls and boys,
she never forgave me forever after.
And I never forgave her for that.

CURSES

Benny was a real burro in school,
but always thought he was better.
One thing though, is true: he didn't hardly cuss.
So he (but I really think his mother
was behind it; this required smarts)
came up with an idea to rid us of the habit forever:
whoever cussed would get punched by each of us
ten times on the shoulder, as hard as possible.
Trouble was that every time somebody got hit,
he would curse even more, scream
¡Cabrón! in pain, or ¡Jodido! in anger,
and of course, the more we cursed
the more we got hit, and the more we got hit, etc.
We were forced to switch shoulders
and finally had to scrap the game altogether.
It got to where we walked
entire blocks in silence.

FREDDY

It was Freddy (who else?) who took a piece of rabbit fur
to school and placed it over his crotch during class.
Freddy, who in the seventh grade chain-smoked Pall Malls
all the way home, and all the way
home talked about Dolores,
slipping her a little, just a little, Spanish fly.
And always that old story about the girl
who was given some
and was found the following morning
impaled on the gearshift of her boyfriend's pickup.
The day of the painful TB shots, we all had to endure
ten punches by everybody on the arm—Freddy's idea.
On the way home everyday was the pinball machine
at Chávez's Grocery where with a nickel
and a piece of hanger,
we'd play for hours, thanks to Freddy, the holes he bored.
Old Chávez would look up suspiciously
from behind the counter as the machine cling-clanged,
popped, popped game after free game.
One day, we walked in to find tin plates installed
along both sides of the machine,
and Freddy the rest of the way home muttered
something about that huge magnet in his garage,
the possibility of breaking in at night
with a hand drill and a quarter-inch metal bit.

GENEVIEVE

Genevieve wore makeup and had a streak of white
in her hair when we were in the seventh grade.
She acted as if she was a woman
of the, and in her, forties. Barbara Stanwyck perhaps.
Always wore brand new and always tight sweaters
and skirts, a bright scarf smartly around her neck.
She was in love with me, madly,
and was always after Benny to find out if I loved her, too.
Promised him fifty cents to get me to say yes.
Benny first tried begging, then bribery, then
resorted to threatening my life constantly for a week.

FINGERS

Benny was always asking what we would do if
the girl we were lucky enough to undress
turned out to be a boy instead.
And asked which fingers we dipped in holy water
to make the sign of the cross
and then which same three to throw a finger.
Always dreamed of driving a Jaguar
and held his nose high as if he owned one.
One day after school, we walked downtown with him
to buy his shoes for the May crowning,
and his socks, his socks, God, his socks,
so caked and stiff.

DOLORES

Dolores, Dolores we discussed your body
on the way home from school. Every day,
Freddy dreamed: a speck of Spanish fly in your cherry Coke.
All talk. Eighth graders.
Nineteen fifty-seven or -eight.
Not a good year for any—especially
a Catholic school girl—to get pregnant.
After that your life is a secret.
What was it you wrote about Sister Ann
on the walls of the girls' bathroom?
She said she recognized your handwriting.

CARDINAL MINDSZENTY

Cardinal Mindszenty.
Perhaps I should say a prayer for you today.
Dead at eighty-five.
The nuns praised you every morning of the eighth grade
when the Communists
were throwing people into meat grinders,
and the only record I had enough nerve to dance to was
"Blueberry Hill."
In complete and total exile from your beloved Hungary.
I remember Ginger's body in a tight skirt;
just looking could cause you to commit a hundred sins.
Hero of a war we never understood.
I never learned to jitterbug.
Every morning we prayed for peace in the world.
One morning before Mass, José told me his grandmother
had cursed the governor and his commodities
in her dying breath.
I wore a black leather jacket.
Perhaps I should have said a prayer for you today.
One o'clock. Two o'clock. Three o'clock rock.

MIRACLES I

We were taught to believe in miracles:
Water into wine
and bread and wine to body and blood.
In these and many others, we believed.
I always prayed that some homework with my name
would somehow appear in the pile.
I suppose I did not believe strongly enough.
I believe I saw two Oriental men
from Duncan Yo-yo downtown one day.
They did the harder tricks like Three Leaf Clover
as easily as Rocking the Cradle,
Round the World, easy stuff.
One of them spun two yo-yos
loop, loop, looploop at the same time.
The other spun his and let it go,
high as the ceiling of Walgreen's it flew
and came down just as quickly, sliding ssffft right, yes,
right into the right-hand pocket of his royal blue blazer.

MIRACLES II

After the movies on Saturday afternoons
we would walk back home down the main street,
by way of the factory, stop
in front of the window, watch
the endless line of Coke bottles
come down the conveyor belt.

Even after Roy Rogers and Trigger, the world
so full of miracles on that side of town.

MARTIN

Our play wagons loaded after a month of collecting,
we headed down the hill to Patsy's father's
junkyard to sell scrap iron.
Patsy had freckles, a fourth-grade love.
Perhaps her father would treat me well
at the mention of her name.
The nuns had stressed so much the importance of honesty.
When Martín suggested throwing in a few extra pieces
lying around the junkyard shed, I was tempted.
Patsy's father noticed, of course,
but Martín denied, denied, denied
and after the weighing came away rich.
True, he had taken more,
but not that much. No matter.
It was becoming quite clear
that it was the Martíns of this world
who own this world.

SISTER CODY

Sister Cody wore a wedding ring, was married
to God, she said. She marched us everywhere,
pulled our ears when we were out of line.
She slapped me once in the sixth grade,
in the name of the Father, the Son.
Those who protested too strongly
were blasphemers, fit only for public school,
so I said nothing,
even pretended to like her,
innocently believing that if I turned
the other cheek, she would too.
Truth is, she never did.
And of the Holy Spirit, Amen.

PATTY

It was love for a month or so in the eighth grade. Patty.
Even got into a fight in the bathroom
over who would dance with her.
Her mother attractive and an Anglo.
Her father made the front page in our seventh-grade year
for arranging abortions. The nuns called for forgiveness.
I saw her again, years later, downtown.
I had a ticket for a free meal, compliments of the U.S. Army,
before boarding a train for basic training.
She told me, more so with her eyes, I should be careful.
I would like to think we had more to say,
but she was quickly gone, another secretary
in the noon-hour crowd returning to work.
She had learned about cheated hopes, corruption,
anguish, and upheaval long before there was a country
in southwest Indochina, divided.

THE PACHUCO'S WEDDING

We were not the little boys and girls of God
we believed, dear God, ourselves to be
that day we marched into church to pray
still another rosary for another special intention.
So strange to see them in church and on a weekday.
We stared.
Her tattooed hand holding nervously fresh flowers
and he in a new suit only he could make look zoot.
It was they who were afraid.
They were on our turf now.

JENNY

Jenny, who was invisible except for the day she lined up
for tetherball, and won, and kept on winning.
And then Sister Ann, the principal, Oh My God!, stepped in.
But she, too, lost. The ball hit too quickly,
fiercely for her.
Jenny, so quiet. Her brothers, also blonde and fair,
were mean pachucos, feared.
Then the bell ended the noon hour,
and Jenny finished that eighth-grade year,
the last anybody would know of her,
silently, somewhere in the last row.

JOE

Sister Ann despised the taps on Joe's shoes.
Said he sounded like a racehorse
walking up the aisle to receive communion.
(They were horseshoe taps.)
One day Joe noticed she too wore taps.
She said it was to honor God,
make her shoes last.
A vow of poverty.
Joe never vowed to be poor.
He simply was.
But did vow to be cool just the same.

EVELYN

Though Sister Ruth had spoken to us about Saint Rita
sending her lovely eyes to her admirer on a platter
in order to better serve God and never again worry
about such earthly distractions,
we still thought that Evelyn,
who limped, wore frilly dresses,
her long hair in curls, colorful ribbons,
and so skinny, was, except for her two older sisters,
the ugliest girl in the whole wide world.

MANUEL

The only time I recall Manuel saying anything bad
about anybody was when Sister Ann told him
his pachuco hairstyle looked like a bird's nest.
We would steal Cokes from the delivery truck, sip them
like gentlemen of leisure on his porch after school
as he strummed his twelve-string guitar, sang corridos.
One night, he and some others broke into a grocery store,
and Manuel, who was always so polite, was the last one out.
The only name the cops got out of him was his own.
Twelve years later, when I saw him for the first time since,
he told me how hard finding jobs had been.
The cost of groceries getting higher and higher.

GEORGY

You would have to say flaco at least twice
to describe how skinny Georgy was.
He looked as if he never had enough to eat,
which could have been the case.
But, man did he do the bebop that day
Sister Ann (of all people) decided
to let us hold a dance in her class.
Everybody brought their 45's:
Fats Domino, Chuck Berry, Bill Haley, Little Richard.
The boys lined up along one side of the room,
and, of course, the girls on the other.
Then Georgy got up to dance with Josie.
But even after that, the boys still on one side.
The girls on the other.
Everybody either afraid or ashamed to dance
in front of Sister.
Finally, she ordered the desks back into place,
mad as the devil.

MRS. WALSH

That year I was in Mrs. Walsh's study hall, second period.
Though I had failed math, I could compute
batting averages, slugging percentages, ERA's.
I studied some Latin, read *Street & Smith's*
baseball magazine, learned as much about baseball as I could
every day out of the encyclopedias.
She let Richard and me talk, as long as we whispered,
and we talked baseball. He was a lefty, played first,
and chewed huge wads of bubble gum.
We could even talk baseball with her.
She wanted to be a friend and was,
though she probably never knew it.
She gave me a ride home once,
but I had her let me off on the main street,
then walked the rest of the way, down the alley.
She had wanted to see where I lived, understand me.
That was the year Grandma died,
and Buddy Holly, Ritchie Valens, the Big Bopper.
The year baseball was born.
I had yet to learn to let myself be loved.

KENNY

Kenny had found a way to spare himself
the agony of endless hours of kneeling
during retreat: basketball knee pads.
But if Sister Ann should find out.
We watched enviously, laughing sneakily
among ourselves every time he turned around,
and smiled blissfully, as if being assumed
into Heaven.

MITCH

Mitch, with only one good hand, his right,
packed all his books home in a briefcase.
He was tall enough to play basketball
and could hold on to one quite well
when we played take away during the lunch hour,
the game stopping whenever his glasses would go flying,
spinning across the playground pavement.
He was chosen over the other candidates, all girls,
to crown the Blessed Virgin in May;
even though he lived the farthest, he walked to Mass daily.
A fastballer, he would settle his glove
on his withered left hand,
wind up, and throw, then slip the glove on, field
a hot grounder, quickly
rip the glove off, find the ball,
and throw to first.
But never quickly enough for coach.

BOBBY

Bobby got his mouth washed out with soap
and water by Sister Ann
in the boys' bathroom in the sixth grade for cussing,
though I'm sure he cussed a lot less than we did.
He did, however, try just as hard to bust the street lamp
near his house after school one day,
rock after rock for an hour.
In the seventh, Sister Stella praised
his kindness and generosity
but wished Heaven would help him
show more interest in school.
Sister Ann treated him as if he had no sense at all, a burro,
even though, or perhaps because, he was an Anglo,
never gave or forgave him a chance,
and failed him in the eighth.
The truth is he showed us the world
through his microscope,
got us interested in Mr. Wizard, taught us
how Lon Chaney transformed himself into the monsters
we watched religiously late, late
Friday nights on *Horror Theater*.
He had read somewhere that in the twenty-first century
the elbow would be considered erotic, taboo.

TIMMY

Debonair was the word Timmy craved,
along with handsome.
He wore a brown leather jacket with a fur collar,
a white scarf tied just so, hair perfectly parted.
A tube of chapstick constantly in and out of his pocket.
The way he chewed his cinnamon-flavored toothpick:
perhaps he had seen an old Bogart movie.
Surprisingly, he'd pull a stolen lemon out of his jacket
a block or so after our daily stop at Montgomery's Grocery.
Not exactly the sweet little boy
his mother believed him to be.
He thought he was what the girls desired.
In the ninth grade, he got his sweetheart pregnant
and left town faster than the rumor of it,
never to be heard from since.
About a year and a half ago,
the Santa Fe Railroad tore down the giant smokestack
that had stood all our lives
across the street from his house.

LAS PIOJOCITAS

Everybody said they were full of piojos,
the three Sánchez sisters, las piojocitas.
They smoked; gossip had it they drank
so very likely they did it too.
Their mother reportedly knew a lot of men.
The rest of the neighborhood girls
would have nothing to do with them.
They wore tight skirts, bright sweaters,
junk jewelry, put on brash eyeliner,
an extravagant lunar, ruby red lipstick,
and arched their eyebrows boldly,
teased their hair high.
They looked like the rock stars of today,
who imagine themselves as wild and as tough.

STEVIE

Because we were born to get our asses kicked
Stevie said
Rule Number One of the barrio was
never let anyone
do it for free,
otherwise he will think it is his
to kick
whenever
and forever.

MIKEY

One day on my way back from lunch,
I stopped by for Mikey
and got a lesson I hadn't counted on.
He was quiet, and so polite.
His sister was beautiful.
I'd impress her.
He hit me with jabs, bewildering hooks, uppercuts.
He also had the sense to have mercy.
The walls of his living room bare
except for a pair of old, wrinkled
boxing gloves dangling from a nail.

SANGRE TAN PESADA

All I can remember about my aunt, poor aunt
her house always so full of flies
(Uncle, it seems, never made enough money
to support in-laws, her children, theirs.
I would never eat there when he visited.),
and how she in her perplexed, polite manner
so nonchalantly said how unbelievingly vain
I was that Sunday I sat insolently outside,
pretending to be deaf to her
ever so many generous invitations.

HOT TAR

Surely there was something easier
than being a stepfather to me.
Love was never allowing
me to work on flat roofs.
Shingles only.
The one battle I never won.
We have luck if we have fathers
who fall from heights we'll never
attain, who wear the scars
left by hot tar day after day.

PADRINO

Uncle Leo, my padrino, was the very best of uncles.
He must have given me a million haircuts.
A quiet man, a boxing champion in the Army,
but I never knew him to use violence,
spoke to me harshly only once.
His advice always: be careful,
learn to be yourself.
I listened, in complete agreement.
But I seemed determined to undo my life.
Uncle Leo, who taught me how to use a saw.
Never, he said, go against the grain.

IMAGINING MYSELF

I wanted a bike, but an old one like the rest
of the guys, the kind their fathers bought
down at the police auction. Instead,
my mother had a Montgomery Ward truck
drive up with a brand-new one—purple.
To make matters worse, she added a basket.
And a nameplate.
Made it practically impossible to be cool.
And then a horn.
I also had a coonskin cap, a fringe jacket.
Even a Davy Crockett garbage can.
I sang "Davy, Davy Crockett, the king of the wild frontier"
all day long, saw the movie twice,
imagined myself grinning at "bars,"
fighting Indians, going to congress.
Even fought Mexicans at the Alamo
to make America free.

JOHNNY

What a better friend than Johnny.
Trouble was he was a first cousin,
from my mother's second set of in-laws
so naturally she didn't like him.
We lived next door to each other,
walked home together
until the last possible moment,
then he went down the alley
and I down the street,
hoping my mother wouldn't notice
(she never failed not to).
He taught me to swim.
About babies.
How to make change
when we sold the *Tribune* downtown.
And how to make a Dr. Pepper fizz
by dropping a peanut
or a pebble in the bottle
outside Benjamín's Grocery.

BENJAMIN

Benjamín, along with his stingy wife,
owned the corner grocery and gas station.
Not many items to choose from.
Seven days a week he wore his green work khakis
and always smelled of kerosene or gas.
Jigsaw puzzle patches of white
scattered over his face and arms.
A hook he used just like a left hand.

FIDO

Fido was famous for a while in the sixth grade:
his appendectomy. Showed me his scar
behind his house one day. An OK friend.
In the seventh, he threw himself on the floor,
humped frantically, and was back on his feet
before Sister Mary made her way up the stairs.
That year he announced he would commit suicide
after school, let a car run him over.
Everybody showed up, taunted as he walked
into traffic, stood safely on the yellow line,
or else stood, eyes closed, valiantly ready
for death, as if unaware he hadn't quite
stepped into the danger of the street,
was just safe enough in front of a parked car.
In the eighth, Josie happened to turn around
when he called Arturo,
and turned red as Sister Ann,
whose face was the color
of chile pequín when she lost her temper.
Got to see Fido's dick before he hid it,
frightened, quickly behind his catechism.

PATSY

It was a good Friday that Friday after school.
A Friday or two before Good Friday.
The saints wrapped in purple
and could not see us out behind the church
after the stations of the cross,
as Patsy, tall enough to be an eighth grader
and certainly prettier, kissed and hungrily
kissed the boys, this boy, this boy, the boys
of St. Francis Xavier.

JANE

The girls weren't allowed to wear nylons
so every morning of the ninth grade,
Sister Ruth would go up and down the aisles
feeling their legs, spurning angrily our offers of help.
Jane had legs skinny as ballpoint pens.
Even the smallest size of nylons hung loosely, wrinkled.
Nevertheless, every morning
found Sister having to send her out of the room.
Otherwise, she was everything a good Catholic school girl
should have been.

FELIPE

Felipe lived not ten feet from the railroad tracks.
His house trembled.
Suddenly, when we started high school,
he began walking to and from with his older sister,
under her watchful eye,
and never went by his first name,
and never talked to us again.
I thought about him today when I heard
the long whistle of the afternoon outbound.
How we envied his collection of miniature swords
he fashioned by placing nail after furtive nail
on the rails for the passing locomotives to flatten.

JIM

The way I heard the story Jim got his white hair quite early,
working as a chemist in a dynamite factory
before he arrived in New Mexico from as far away as Iowa.
Jim, who never married (there were whispers he was queer).
He lived (they said) in a room surrounded by books.
Thin, frail, and bespectacled.
Jim, who smiled kindly, warned me
I should learn to be careful.
I was eighteen or so then,
but it would take me another eighteen
and more to begin to understand.
It was Jim who introduced me to the university.
He was certain the government had been infiltrated
by the Communists and gave me right-wing books to read.

SISTER ANN

Sister Ann had us pray for Mother Seton's canonization.
And for Mother Cabrini.
We sang the Marine Corps hymn.
And another song:
"You always know your neighbor
You always know your pal
if you've ever navigated
on the Erie Canal."
She read J. Edgar Hoover and warned us, fervently
hoped we would pray Red China never
be allowed into the UN.
She lectured about equality and injustice.
Discrimination against Catholics
cost Al Smith the presidency.
Lord, she wondered, why had she been sent
out west from Cincinnati to teach here,
in the land of mañana, always mañana.

RAMON

Haircuts at Ramón's were fifty cents
and just across the arroyo.
Downtown was across the tracks,
out of the question.
He had a barber's chair
but no license.
The State was constantly
closing him down.

He swore he had seen us
down in the arroyo with some girls,
doing things I asked
Benny to explain
on the way home, but he couldn't always.

Knowing his wife was in the kitchen,
he told us dirty jokes,
pressing himself strangely
against us.

BENNY

All that summer Benny
masturbated
under the old bridge.
Every day,
trying to beat time.
A pocket watch in the other hand.

CASTILLO

Castillo, our scoutmaster claimed
he grew prize calabazas in Colorado.
Vines so long they crossed the highway.
So thick the traffic couldn't crush them.
He let us stone a rattler once.
Told us never urinate on a fire,
the smoke crawls up your penis,
damages your liver.
Once, swimming in a large pond,
his vine slipped out of his shorts.

TIMMY'S BROTHER

Timmy's brother worked in the beauty shop downtown.
Never bothered to talk to us when we stopped by
with Timmy on our way home from school.
He thought that he,
and he only, could be considered beautiful.
Dyed his brown hair bright blonde
and had an Anglo boyfriend
that he brought to the barrio one day.
Benny said it was too bad none of the older pachucos
were around to pull down his pants,
see if he was true blonde down below, too.

DAVY

One day Davy whispered the way he had never before.
Something he wanted to show me in his aunt's bedroom
where he took out her big, black brassiere.
Halloween came, and the neighborhood boys
tripped and stumbled
down streets, alleys in our mothers' old dresses,
wearing lipstick, rouge, cursing.
His idea.

TEDDY

We were walking down Central downtown,
and Teddy said to me, the way older guys
say something when teaching you this and that,
said don't give the Anglo girls the eye,
the satisfaction.
He turned me on to Cannonball, Bird, Brubeck: Time Out.
When I returned from Vietnam, he played
Bach's "Minuet in G Minor" for me on his rock 'n roll guitar
then put on "Love For Sale"
and smiled to himself, entranced
as he played it over, over, over, and over.
Next day I didn't have to read past the *Tribune* headlines
to know it was he who had beaten
his mother to death with a hammer in 5/4 time.

TURO

Everybody advised against a fight with Turo.
That I know of he was not the type to pick one,
minded his business and so mild mannered
you thought he might be easy to beat.
He was muscular, had handsome black hair, deep dark eyes,
and didn't appear capable of sudden madness.
According to the story, he had overturned a tub
of boiling water on himself as a child,
was driven insane, and ever since
he would probably kill if he was so much as touched.
Or something crazy like that.

SUSANNA

Susanna suddenly became a neighbor
one summer next door.
Instantly all the boys liked her, as did I,
but from afar, and long after the rest.
I was also in love with Susan Hayward:
that color photo of her in my mother's movie magazine.
Her red hair on fire.
Sister Ruth explained to us once the torment
of the fires of hell. It was the soul, not the flesh,
that burned, and forever. Forever.
I was only twelve or so and bursting into flames.

HECTOR

Hector had huge biceps, a pompadour, lifted tons
of weights daily. Impressed himself,
the young boys of the neighborhood.
Parents urged caution.
Slow in every way and an epileptic as well,
he was said to be dangerous,
perfectly capable of going totally
out of control.
And of very little else.

ALICE

Alice, poor as nobody else,
and pretty,
(well, somewhat)
was a first kiss.
I thought it might be more
(she was said to).
But no.
In my first car, a '51 Chevy
as dark brown as she was.

FRIEDA

Frieda back in the fifties. One day
her boyfriend, in black denims, white T-shirt,
sleeves rolled up, hair greased back,
cigarette dangling, surly, I suppose, behind his shades,
picked her up after school, in his black Ford, top down,
a miracle, we were sure, if it went up,
and she, frivolously, tossed her books, jumped in
so he could varoom off, leave us ninth grade boys in awe,
though no one considered her even close to pretty,
but the car wouldn't start and wouldn't start,
and we stood around waiting, amused,
and the Ford wouldn't start, and Frieda frozen,
saying to herself (I'm sure), This would happen to me,
wouldn't start, wouldn't start, and Frieda's boyfriend
pressing, pressing the button, staying cool, cool,
but it wouldn't, and Frieda trying hard not to,
This would, would happen to me,
wouldn't start wouldn't start,
until finally somehow it cranked over, and he peeled out,
tires screeching, muffler roaring, varooming,
leaving us gawking, the way he meant it all to be
in the first place.

TOCAYO

One day suddenly a huge cloud of smoke
down the hill; big, red trucks
came from across town to our side,
lights flashing, sirens, Police, the Sheriff.
The rest of the day parents gossiped.
The dangers of playing with matches.
Oh, to be as famous as my tocayo!
His name traveling faster than the fire itself.

ROYBAL

He owned the corner grocery store on the road
we took only to Mass Sunday mornings
and sometimes home from the movies Saturdays.
We rarely entered.
Supposedly he had spent several years in prison,
though that version of his story
was eventually lost, forgotten along with other gossip.
He had a streak of wild peroxide white through his hair
and spoke as little as possible, careful, always.
Smoked his cigarette slowly, patiently.
And refused credit to everybody.

MONTGOMERY

Montgomery's Cokes were the coldest, in ice water
after school.
The freshest chocolate-covered donuts.
His was the cleanest grocery,
oiled wooden floors covered with fresh sawdust.
Brilliant red tomatoes, lettuce green
as brand-new dollar bills.
He sat behind the counter, smoking his Pall Malls quietly.
Surely he knew.
Or perhaps we were better thieves than we imagined.
Those bright yellow, succulent lemons
about the size, we imagined, of Dolores' breasts.
Truly a shame to steal from him.
An Anglo, after all.

RUMALDO

Rumaldo, his eyes thin squints
behind the thickest of glasses.
Owned a corner grocery.
You could call it typical.
Counters in what should have been
the living room.
His sentences fast, punctuated
by a faster stutter.
It could've been Japanese.
Punched and cranked his adding machine
even faster.
And looked exactly
like Emperor Hirohito.

TONY

The winter I returned from Vietnam
Grandpa told me Tony had been found
frozen to death in his pickup.
It was said he drank a lot; perhaps the mass layoffs.
He was good at marbles; swung an axe
with the strength, precision of somebody twice his age.
His father, I think, had abandoned the family.
In our First Holy Communion photo,
he is holding a candle,
his right hand over his heart,
and smiling, wearing a new suit.
Twenty years later the mines have been closed.

ALL THE DELICIOUS CHERRIES

Some, I'm sure many, would say we were poor.
Grandpa got a green check in the mail.
And the government cheese and butter.
The rice and powdered milk were always full of maggots.
Summer came, and he planted most of the yard with corn
and calabacitas. And he had chickens.
And apple trees.
Grandma planted peas, carrots, radishes, yerba buena.
And there were stories. Always.
Oh, and, a young boy could go out by the chicken coop
all summer long, whenever,
and pick all the delicious cherries that bucket
Grandma had bought full of strawberry jam would hold.

THE HISTORY OF HOME

I turned to Flaco to see if,
but he had no idea either
who this "Sweet Betsy from Pike
who crossed the mountains
with her lover Ike" was,
that day in sixth-period English,
Mrs. Stevens had us sing,
and Flaco and I were the only ones
who didn't know the words.

MIGUEL

According to them his gun was drawn.
They had removed it from the scene, evidence.

His brother standing beside me,
telling me Miguel was a marksman
in the Marines and could've shot any of them.

A cop's bullet exactly between his eyes.

THE SISTERS OF CHARITY

I could never understand the Sisters of Charity.
Why they had so very little
(unless you happened to be a favorite).
They pulled you into line by the ear,
slapped, belittled you. Hard to believe
that the God we prayed to so often
was the one who had sent them.
All they knew was Cincinnati.
Since then, I have hated the Church, and Catholics.
And, except in time of great need,
(Vietnam, for instance),
I have denied the existence of God.
The most and least I can say is that God
is where my words, these words, come from.
And if I still weren't such a stubborn, unforgiving fool,
the one to whom they should be offered.

POINTS NORTH

Sadness was Eddie Fisher crooning
"O mein Papa, to me he was so wonderful . . .
to me he was so good" on the battered jukebox
down at the old bus depot on Second Street
as the loudspeaker announced departures
for Santa Rosa, Tucumcari, points east,
to Grants, Gallup, Flagstaff, and points west.
And then, too soon, time for Grandpa to leave
after returning me to my parents, the end of summer.
The scratched recording announcing the departure
of a Greyhound boarding for Santa Fe, Las Vegas,
Watrous, Wagon Mound, Springer, Raton
(where Grandfather would get off,
walk across the tracks, then up the hill, home),
Trinidad, Walsenburg, Pueblo, Denver, and points north.
All aboard, please.
Suddenly the entire world seemed
as far away and as empty as points north.

EL ARABE

Grandfather called him El Arabe,
the Old Arab, who owned the grocery
at the bottom of the hill on the way to town.
He wore black sleeves fastened by safety pins
over his rumpled, white shirt,
a green gambler's eye shade, round-rimmed, serious glasses,
a long, soiled apron splashed with blood.
Always a day's growth or two of gray stubble.
The white hair of a mad scientist.
He would total the groceries with his good hand, his right,
then pack them as Grandpa complained in Spanish
about his high prices, the nerve of this old cripple.
I'm sure he understood, but his face betrayed nothing.
Somehow Grandpa always had a nickel left over for me.
The Old Arab would drag his left foot
across the oiled wooden floor to the freezer,
grab his left arm, place a cone in the lifeless hand, and dip a
scoop of delicious chocolate-swirled vanilla,
and smile, rub my head affectionately, wink slyly,
as if we belonged to some secret society
that didn't allow grandfathers,
who complained about money, as members.

MAÑANA ME VOY, MAÑANA

When it came time for me
to go live with my parents again,
Grandma would sing those sad lines
"Mañana me voy, mañana,
mañana me voy de aquí,"
the same song I have found myself singing
the many times I've moved.
Smoking her brown-paper cigarrito,
even more incessantly than usual,
she would smile sadly
from across the kitchen, call me her "hijito."
Her eyes, I knew, teary and red already
behind the sunglasses she wore only then,
or when we walked down the hill
and across the tracks to town.

BENJIE

A long time has passed since Benjie,
who was our age plus half or more,
who wore dress pants as if he went to school
instead of Mass every day, a step or two behind
his old mother, jaw dangling, eyes bulging
as if amazed always by the same faces,
trees, and houses to and from.
One day we were playing dodgeball
when he came walking by with Donny.
We knew so many, many games,
none he could play or understand, of course,
but the next thing we knew, we were circled
around him, delighted as he pulled his index finger
back, back far enough to break it, Unbelievable!
As easy for him as ten times ten for us.
We pleaded Again, Benjie, Again! and he pulled
his hands from behind his back, bent his finger back again,
his tongue darting out as he lowered his head,
embarrassed, then hid his hands again, and we pleaded
Again! Again! and he bent his finger back,
over and over again, until soon he too was laughing wildly,
and then Donny announced it was time to go,
and time ran again, ran swiftly, and one day
I found myself home again, but, as always, only for a while,
home again asking whatever became of him,
Poor Benjie, whatever
of his mother, who, I learned,
had taken poison, when pregnant
with him after learning of her husband's many mistresses.

THE FORMULAS OF WORDS

It was always the formulas of words I loved best.
I failed arithmetic in the fifth grade.
Never could do long division.
Did surprisingly well in algebra for a while.
Ended up taking plane geometry twice
and got caught reading poetry in back of the classroom.

I never tired of Grandma's stories, Grandpa's adventures.
I would sit on the living room couch after school
entranced by the rhythm, rhyme of the hymns,
stanza after stanza in the back of the catechism.
I read the stories in my uncles' schoolbooks
that Grandma brought down from the attic.
Movies were a quarter (What a deal!)
down at Bustamante's, a double feature plus cartoons.
And of course, comic books, especially the classics
that other kids had trouble trading, except to me.

TRUTH

Mine has always been a silent world.
So words have not been easy.
And words have been easy.
As easy as words.
As another lie; oh, I have lied.
And I have denied.
And then denied that I denied.
I have invented myself so many times
so that others would believe I was who they thought
I was, and I suppose, so that I, too, would believe.
And also for no particular reason.
Oh, I have lied.
And that is the truth.

NOVEMBER TWENTY-SECOND

November twenty-second.
I was nineteen and working as a roofer.
The Moon Street apartments in Albuquerque.
I was shingling a gable.
An elderly woman came from across the street.
She either asked if we knew or else told us.
The president had been shot.
It was about three o'clock.
She mentioned Dallas, a few other things.
Then went back.
Shortly afterwards the chuck wagon came.
I sat on a bundle of shingles, watching
as men below gathered around fires.
My stepfather climbed back up the ladder,
said a black man, a carpenter, told him he'd lost a friend.
He shook his head sadly,
not knowing what else or more to say.
We went back to work, the world now coming apart.
And all the men, and all the nails,
and all the Mexican wetback bricklayers
at a penny a brick,
could never put it back together again.